In
memory
of
Mara Ann
"Bug"
Smith
(12/16/98
-
12/17/00)

# BUZZ

"Aerodynamically speaking, the bumblebee shouldn't be able to fly, but the bumblebee doesn't know it, so it goes on flying anyway."

For Solita and Solita and Mie and Cole—E. S.

To Elise Nguyen—V. N.

SIMON & SCHUSTER BOOKS FOR YOUNG READERS
An imprint of Simon & Schuster Children's Publishing Division
1230 Avenue of the Americas, New York, New York 10020
Text copyright © 2010 by Eileen Spinelli • Illustrations copyright © 2010 by Vincent Nguyen
SIMON & SCHUSTER BOOKS FOR YOUNG READERS is a trademark of Simon & Schuster, Inc.
For information about special discounts for bulk purchases, please contact
Simon & Schuster Special Sales at 1-866-506-1949 or business@simonandschuster.com.
The Simon & Schuster Speakers Bureau can bring authors to your live event.
For more information or to book an event, contact the Simon & Schuster Speakers Bureau at
1-866-248-3049 or visit our website at www.simonspeakers.com.
Book design by Chloë Foglia • The text for this book is set in Golden Cockerel.
The illustrations for this book are rendered in mixed media: painted in oils and Photoshop.
Manufactured in China • 1109 SCP
2 4 6 8 10 9 7 5 3 1
Library of Congress Cataloging-in-Publication Data
Spinelli, Eileen. • Buzz / Eileen Spinelli ; illustrated by Vincent Nguyen.—1st ed. • p. cm.
Summary: After learning that a bee's body is too chunky for flight,
Buzz the bumblebee defies the laws of aerodynamics to save a friend in need.
ISBN 978-1-4169-4925-1 • [1. Bumblebees—Fiction. 2. Flight—Fiction. 3. Animals—Fiction.]
I. Nguyen, Vincent, ill. II. Title. • PZ7.S7566Bu 2010 • [E]—dc22 • 2008042191

# BUZZ

By Eileen Spinelli

Illustrated by Vincent Nguyen

Simon & Schuster Books for Young Readers

NEW YORK    LONDON    TORONTO    SYDNEY

Buzz loved being a bee.

She loved the taste of honey.

She loved dozing in her cozy hive.

She loved nosing in the sunlit clover.

But most of all,

she loved flying!

Sometimes Buzz would swoop real low under the blackberry bramble where Snail lived.

Sometimes Buzz stopped to visit Snail.

Snail, who could not fly, enjoyed hearing Buzz tell about the world beyond her berry bramble.

Buzz would buzz the latest: "Grasshopper got sick eating too much skunk cabbage!"

"Mouse is off visiting her city cousin!"

Sometimes, just before dusk, Buzz would swoop real high to visit Old Owl in his willow tree.

Old Owl always had wise things to say:

"Honey isn't everything."

"Let sleeping owls alone."

One day, when Buzz was out flying, a storm came up. And the wind blew a sheet of newspaper out from under a bench.

The headline caught Buzz's eye.

Buzz flew in for a closer look.

She was shocked as she read the story—

# PROFESSOR DECLARES BEES CAN'T FLY

Professor Emile Popkin's study is complete. He says the body of a bee is too chunky for flight. "Airplanes, birds, and dragonflies are made to fly," he says. "But a bee's chunky body—well, it has no business getting off the ground. And yet

The rest of the article was missing. But Buzz had read enough. If someone like Professor Popkin said bees can't fly—it must be true.

Buzz bobbled.

And wobbled.

And fell—PLIP—to the ground.

Befuddled, she huddled under the brambles.

Snail tried to cheer Buzz. "It's not so bad not being able to fly," she said.

Buzz sniffled. "It is for me!"

Snail offered Buzz a berry blossom.

Buzz was not hungry.

Berry juice?

Buzz was not thirsty.

Buzz sniffed the afternoon air. "I smell smoke."

She peered into the woods and saw a flicker of flame.

"Fire!" she cried. "Old Owl is in there!"

Old Owl was a very sound sleeper.

Nothing ever woke him before dusk.

Buzz had to get to her friend. Fast!

Buzz raced around a fallen pinecone.

Scrambled over a twig.

She stumbled. She tumbled.

She tripped and she flipped.

Old Owl needed her and all she could do was run.

How would she ever get up the tree?

Buzz wished she had never read the professor's words.

The words thumped like her beating heart as she raced over the forest floor.

Bees can't fly! Bees can't fly! Bees can't fly!

I must warn Owl . . . I must warn Owl . . . I must warn Owl . . .

The more she thought of Old Owl, the less she thought of the professor's words.

Until . . .

suddenly . . .

the milkweeds were below her and the firelight
was warm on the buzzing blur of her wings.

## She was flying!

She darted into Old Owl's nest.

Smoke billowed and made her drowsy.

She settled woozily by her friend and

buzzed as loud as she could.

She held that note until she toppled

into Old Owl's ear.

Old Owl awoke with a start.

"Fire!" he cried and swooped from the nest.

He perched in the hollow of a nearby maple tree and waited.

Luckily, it soon began to rain.

Later, when it stopped, Old Owl shook his damp feathers. Then he sneezed.

Out from his ear popped Buzz.

"Buzz!" said Old Owl. "What are you doing in my ear?"

"I think I saved you," said Buzz. "And I can fly!"

"Of course you can fly," said Old Owl. "You're a bee. Bees fly."

"Yes," said Buzz. "You're right. I'm a bee."